Good Food at the Food Truck

By Cecilia Minden

This is a food truck.

A food truck sells good food.

4   **You can get a hot dog.**

This is a hot dog in a bun.

6

You can get a taco.

This is a taco.

Do you want pizza?

You can get pizza.

This food truck sells
apples and plums.

This is an apple.

This is a plum.

A food truck sells good food.

Word List

sight words

a	Do	is	taco
and	food	of	This
apples	good	or	want
are	have	pizza	You

short a words	short e words	short i words	short o words	short u words
at	get	in	dog	bun
can	sells		hot	plum
			on	truck

This is a food truck.

A food truck sells good food.

You can get a hot dog.

This is a hot dog in a bun.

You can get a taco.

This is a taco.

Do you want pizza?

You can get pizza.

This food truck sells apples and plums.

This is an apple.

This is a plum.

A food truck sells good food.

Published in the United States of America by Cherry Lake Publishing
Ann Arbor, Michigan
www.cherrylakepublishing.com

Photo Credits: © MaraZe/Shutterstock.com, cover, 1; © Hong Vo/Shutterstock.com, back cover, 9; © patrimonio designs ltd/Shutterstock.com, 2; © Anna Moskvina/Shutterstock.com, 3; © Charles Brutlag/Shutterstock.com, 4; © Danny E Hooks/Shutterstock.com, 5, 15; © Prostock-studio/Shutterstock.com, 6; © Gregory Gerber/Shutterstock.com, 7; © Andrey Starostin/Shutterstock.com, 8; © traveler1116/iStockphoto, 10 – editorial; © Tim UR/Shutterstock.com, 11; © Kyselova Inna/Shutterstock.com, 12; © Blulz60/Shutterstock.com, 13

Copyright © 2019 by Cherry Lake Publishing

All rights reserved. No part of this book may be reproduced or utilized
in any form or by any means without written permission from the publisher.

Cherry Blossom Press is an imprint of Cherry Lake Publishing.

Library of Congress Cataloging-in-Publication Data has been filed and is available at catalog.loc.gov

Printed in the United States of America
Corporate Graphics

Cecilia Minden is the former director of the Language and Literacy Program at Harvard Graduate School of Education. She earned her PhD in Reading Education at the University of Virginia. Dr. Minden has written extensively for early readers. She is passionate about matching children to the very book they need to improve their skills and progress to a deeper understanding of all the wonder books can hold. Dr. Minden and her family live in McKinney, Texas.